Land of no Return

N.K. Aning

Published by N.K. Aning, 2022.

LAND OF NO RETURN

First edition. March 10, 2022.

Copyright © 2022 N.K. Aning.

ISBN: 979-8201011703

Written by N.K. Aning.

Also by N.K. Aning

Imaginaterium
Pierce and the City of Imaginaterium
Pierce and the Fallen Gods
The legend of Pierce and Peter : The Dawn

Poetry
In Her Eyes
The Agony of Life
A Memory of Death

Short Stories
The Bronze Man's Secret
Jack and God
Jason And The Great Dragon
The State
First Contact
The Agony of a Slave

Table of Contents

To my son, Kyrian

Chapter One
1990

The screams were the worst things he remembered. Brave men reduced to whimpering cowards in the face of horror. From where he crouched in the bamboo foliage, he listened to the dying screams of the last of his friends. It was only a matter of time before they found him. His heart was pounding in his chest, he blinked away the sweat trickling into his eyes. His calf was burning and for the first time, he felt the sting of a wound caused by a spear grazing his calf. His friends had died like livestock in that place. He sniffed, Jack O'Connor, famed hunter extraordinaire, reduced to a coward who abandoned his friends. He choked back the tears threatening to overwhelm him.

What had he gotten himself into? He could still hear the drumming in his hiding place. There was little visibility under the light from the moon. He breathed a sigh of relief when the echoes of the drumming faded into the distance. A monkey screeched above him startling him. He stepped out of the foliage, squinting and exhaling to calm his beating heart. Jack did the sign of the cross. A twig snapped behind him. His heart lurched in his chest. *How had he gotten himself into this?* The world would never know the truth and that caused him to sob even more. Another twig snapped and his eyes bulged. He had seen how his friends had died. He felt something hot flush against his thigh. A pool formed beneath him, and he began to cry as he felt a presence behind him. His screams echoed all over the forests as the monkeys screeched in fear above him.

Chapter Two
2000

"Mom, this is boring," Ethan said while ruffling his golden hair. Beside him, his sister Emily Brown was making faces at him.

"Ethan, we'll be out here soon. Just stay calm." His mom, Claudette said as she snapped photos of some exotic birds. The Australians had been touring the jungles of Uganda. They had made a pit stop at the Kampala Hotel and having heard of the jungle decided to visit it.

Ethan rolled his tongue at his sister while wiping the sweat from his brow. He wondered why they could not just stay in their hotel. He wished to be back home. Mom and her stupid holiday tours, he thought as his attention was drawn to his sister beckoning him backwards. He scowled, knowing his sister was up to no good. He stole a glance at his mother and saw her still engrossed in taking photos of insects. *Why grown-ups were fascinated by some stuffs was still a mystery to him?* He followed his sister.

"Where are you going?" He whispered as they ventured deeper into the jungle.

"Shh!" Emily shushed him, placing a dirty finger on his lips.

"We're going to play a game," she said with a wink.

Ethan smiled, pleased at his sister's comment. The whole day had been boring. As they walked deeper into the forest, they could hear the steady thrum of the waterfall. Twigs cracked as they made their way towards a cave. Through the tickets, the peak of Mount Elgon could be seen.

"Emily, I think we should go back," Ethan said, voice faltering.

"You're not chickening out on me now bro." Emily said with a smug face.

Ethan knew he did not want to look scared in front of his sister, "fine!" He said even as his heart pounded like crazy.

They entered the cave and Ethan switched on his penlight, a gift from his grandfather. The light bounced off the cave walls revealing very detailed paintings. The children were mesmerized. Far off in the distance they could hear their names being called. The kids ventured deeper into the cave and came to a dead end. A drawing of a warrior like person was on the cave wall.

"What do you think it is?" Emily asked, gazing at the ancient painting.

"I don't know. Looks like an alien to me."

"Boys and movies," she said, casting a sidelong glance at her brother and shaking her head.

Ethan studied the painting and felt his shin crawling with goosebumps. "We need to go back Emily." He whispered, casting a furtive glance backwards. He could not see the entrance of the cave from where they were. They must have wondered off.

"Just a moment," Emily said as she moved closer to the painting. Ethan cast a worried look backwards and stepped beside his sister.

"What are you—"

"Shh!"

She pointed at the painting. Ethan eyes focused on her fingers and saw what she was pointing at. A tiny cleft was installed halfway above the painting of the warrior. Ethan mopped the sweat on his brow and he stiffened as he saw Emily moved closer to the painting.

"Stop!" he shouted, "You have no idea what that would do." He grabbed her hand.

She twisted free and pushed the cleft.

"Noo!"

Nothing happened. They both stood there for a minute glancing at each other.

"Well, it was worth a try."

"Mom will hear of this." Ethan said in disbelief as he turned and began to walk away.

"Chic—"

A grating sound could be heard coming from right in front of them. They both stopped in their tracks, eyes wide.

"What was that?" Emily squeaked as she scooted closer to her brother and held his hands. Proximity did nothing as their bodies trembled. They slowly turned around and stared at the dead end of the cave. Only that it wasn't a dead end anymore. They shone their light at the hole and both children screamed.

Chapter Three
Present day

"Professor, are you really sure this is a good idea?" Susan asked while staring through the window of the plane. Her guts clenched when the plane was hit by turbulence.

Professor Jones Harrison, a man with a salt and pepper beard expelled a tired breath. He adjusted his cowboy hat before dignifying her with a response.

"How many times must we go through this? Don't you want to earn your doctorate?" Jones gazed at her with an arched eyebrow.

Susan could not believe she had been talked into accompanying her professor on this journey. While he admired Jones for his extensive knowledge in history, he was an insufferable tutor who always had his way. Jones smiled at her and pulled the hat over his face, obviously signaling her that he wanted to doze off.

Susan cast her eyes around the occupants of the plane. Jack Quainoo sat on the right going through some magazines. He gave her a wink when he saw her staring at him again. She quickly pulled her eyes away and focused on the two teenagers with their heads together listening to music through their earpiece. They were a five-member team. How the professor had managed to coax the university to fund such a venture was an enigma to her?

"We will be landing very soon. Please fasten your seat belts." Everyone stirred at the voice of the pilot. Susan fastened her seat belt as she felt the plane banked steadily downwards. She felt trepidation build in her gut. She had never enjoyed flying and this was her third flight.

Through the window she gazed at the runway lights. She braced herself and prayed.

They passed through the checkpoints swiftly and boarded a taxi. A hotel had already been booked for their stay. Her room was beside Jones with the two teenagers on the far end. She was too tired to bother with removing her dress and flung herself unto the queen size bed. She gazed up at the chandeliers. Just when she begun to doze off, she recalled she had to take a shower. She stepped into the bathroom and let the cold-water slide over her body. A mirror on the bathroom wall showed her dimpled dark face staring back at her. She had bags under her eyes. She needed to get more sleep. She flung herself naked unto the bed and was asleep in minutes.

PROFESSOR JONES HARRISON sat behind a mahogany desk in his hotel room. His sight was glued to the newspaper clipping he held in his hand. The aesthetic beauty of the room in which he was lodged in was of no concern to him. Being a professor of history, he had the luxury of studying the historical impacts of different eras. He had been composing an essay on Emperor Nero and his fixation with Christendom. He had stumbled across an interesting news item online when he had been doing some research for his lectures. He held the newspaper he had pleaded with a colleague to mail to him. He read the extract again.

"Two kids, a brother and a sister were found outside a cave in the region of Mount Elgon. Kids were blabbering about seeing a giant white ghost in the cave. They described symbols which made no sense whatsoever. Authorities have cordoned off the area to visitors until investigation have been carried out and the truth ascertained....."

Jones scratched his head and read the story over again. His old but intelligent mind was unto something. He fished out his own brown book and opened to the myths and history of Uganda. He glanced at his watch. He had little over six hours to sleep. He put on his spectacles and began to read.

SUSAN WOKE UP WITH a blinding light in her vision. She had forgotten to close the drapes in her room and sun rays was streaming in. She showered and donned a jeans with a pink top emblazoned with 'I love my self.' She walked out her room with her backpack. She had come prepared. She descended the stairs and heard commotion downstairs as she approached the reception where they had agreed to meet. Professor Jones was arguing with a short plump lady. Behind her were her two kids making faces at the professor. The receptionist was at a loss as to how to separate the two. Susan got closer to them and coughed.

Immediately the arguments stopped. Jones turned to Susan and smiled. "Hey, I was just explaining—" He paused, a slight tick in his jaw, "to this lady here that the first ride was ours." Jones said as he gazed expectantly at Susan for support.

Susan's gaze switched between the professor and the plump lady who had her arms crossed. Jones obviously wanted her to choose his side. Her lips curled up as she remembered how the professor had tricked her into coming with him on this journey if she wanted to earn her doctorate. She pretended to think about it.

"Prof, why don't we wait for the next car?" Susan said while smiling sweetly at him. Jones scowled, saying nothing. "Afterall, these kids want to be out of here, right?" the kids eagerly nodded their heads.

"Agreed?"

"Of course." Jones said, accepting defeat graciously, his eyes belying his anger.

"Of course, no thanks to you." The woman said whirling around on her high heeled shoe as her kids followed her.

"How rude," Susan paused as she saw the calculating eye the professor was giving her.

"You just had to ruin that. Didn't you? I know you did it on purpose."

"No! I would never—"

Jones put on his hat, "never mind. I'll make some calls to an old friend of mine." He moved aside as he began to engage someone on his walkie talkie like phone.

Susan was amused and turned to the receptionist who was pretending to be seriously staring at something on his computer. She heard something being dragged and someone giggling. She rolled her eyes and saw the two teenagers, Chloe and Mark appeared, dragging a suitcase behind them. As predictable as ever. They were the youngest in the group. Susan still could not comprehend how the professor had gotten permission to let them tag along. Another thought popped into her mind; did they sleep in the same room? With the way they acted around each other, it was safe to assume both had been doused in a love potion.

"Hey Susan."

Susan's thought was cut off as Jack Quainoo came into view. He was tall and extremely built like an athlete. There was something about him Susan couldn't put her hand on. She smiled back at him.

"Sleep well?" She said as she gazed up at his ruggedly handsome face. She knew he was overly protective of her, but he didn't really show any active romantic interest.

"Yea, a bit," he said in a deep voice. Jack had a commanding presence in any room. She knew the girls in her class ogled him anytime he lectured. "Where is the old man?" Jack asked, a smile twitching on his lips at the joke. He was the professor's assistant so he could afford to call him that.

Susan shrugged and stopped short as she saw the professor approaching them and grinning.

"Ok, guys I've got good news. We will be escorted by our very own local guide."

"Any moment from now," Jones said, staring at the door of the hotel lobby. They all stared in anticipation. The door opened and a figure walked in. Susan felt her mouth opening in shock as they all stared at the person before them.

Chapter Two

The jeep was hot as the team drove towards the caves close to Mount Elgon. Susan drank a bottle of water to quench her thirst. The heat was terrible even as she tried to roll down the window of their jeep. The jeep's air conditioning was faulty. Professor Jones sat at the front with their local guide who was as handsome as a Hollywood star. He was regaling the professor with some tales of the cave.

Susan was sandwiched between Jack and Mark, his camera bouncing off his knees. Mark was there to chronicle their journey yet seemed to be more enamored of Chloe. Behind them another jeep was carrying the other team members plus a model called Joana. She was with her crew to take some photographs. From her window, Susan could see Mount Elgon. Restaurants had sprung up around the area to accommodate the influx of tourist to the place each year. The jeep came to a stop in front of the Mount Elgon Lodge. Susan got out and stretched her legs, lessening the cramps in her thighs from sitting for too long.

"Nice place, isn't it?" Jack said as he came to stand beside her. He had his backpack behind him. "I definitely hope they serve good food here," Jack said winking at Susan. "My stomach is growling."

Their guide, Joseph Muku laughed. "My brother, I can assure you that Ugandan cuisine is the best."

Jack clicked his tongue and arched an eyebrow. "You've not tasted Jollof from Ghana. I assure you my brother, you will want to become a Ghanaian."

Professor Jones laughed as he shook his head.

Susan glared at the two of them and scowled. "If you're done comparing dicks, can we go and get something to eat?"

Jack chuckled as Joseph Muku did a perfunctory bow. "Of course, madam Susan, I'll take the lead." Joseph said as he beckoned the team to follow him.

The group followed the guide to the lodge. They were shown to a table. A bit far from them the model Joana was posing and taking photos.

Susan shook her head. Not that she was jealous. Maybe jealous. Who wouldn't want to have that slim, sexy body men always fawned over? The near perfect skin.

"Hey!" Jack said, snapping Susan from her reverie. "Won't you dig in or you want to be fed?" he said this with a teasing glint in his eye. Susan blushed.

Susan took a bite out of her food and moaned. "Wow, this is good."

"Of course, this is good," Joseph said, shooting a meaningful look towards Jack. "It's our national dish. Only expect the best from Uganda, my princess."

Susan arched an eyebrow at the compliment. It felt good to be appreciated. The professor was reading a newspaper and eating his food.

"Muku," Jones said, "tell me what you know about the story of the two Australians?"

Susan paused with her food halfway to her mouth. She noticed a momentary look of confusion on Joseph's face, but it was immediately wiped off by his usual chatty demeanor. Outside the sun had set.

"It's just an old wives' tale."

Jones frowned, stroking his salt and pepper beard. "You're saying there no truth to what the children saw?"

Joseph chuckled but Susan saw something else in his eyes. "You believe a monster lives in the cave?" They all chuckled at the table. Outside they could hear drums and songs being played.

"Waiter!" Joseph Muku said as they stood up and followed him to an area where there was a bon fire and a local dance was being enacted.

"What's that?" Susan said, fascination drawing her closer to the dancing.

"Professor, do you want to do the honours?" Joseph said, deferring to the professor. Susan rolled her eyes. Jones always wanted an audience to perform to and now he had one.

Jones tipped his hat to them, "the dance is a recreation of the creation by Ruhanga from the Bunyoro myth."

"I thought the Bunyoro myth was just a legend?" Chloe asked, confusion etched on her face.

"Myth alright," Jones said. A bit far from them, the dancers were moving around a man playing the role of Ruhanga. "But every myth holds a grain of truth albeit small."

"But Chloe is right," Susan said, forehead creasing as the light from the bon fire reflected in her eyes. Mark jabbed Chloe playfully as she blushed. "These creation myths were used to explain natural phenomenon. Take the Greek myths for instance."

Jones scowled and shook his head, hands ruffling through his grey hair. He seemed to be lost in thought, staring at the bon fire. The rhythm of the drums was so mournful.

"Prof?" Susan said, jolting Jones out of his thoughts. Susan shared a look with the rest of the team who shrugged.

Jones smiled, a resigned look on his face. "The Bunyoro myth might have been the imagination of some long dead Bacchwesi but there was an empire of Kitara no doubt."

"The empire of Kitara," Jack whispered almost reverently as Susan scowled at him.

"But I'm sure our guide here knows more about the Bunyoro myth than this old man here," said Jones, a wry smile on his face as everyone chuckled.

Joseph Muku took center stage, winking at Jack who scowled. The group was sitting down in a semi-circle. Susan noticed Jack had scooted closer to her and had his arms around her.

"In the creation story, Ruhanga..."

Susan placed her head on Jack's shoulder and imagined the gods of the Bunyoro Myth as Ruhanga took on the form of Muku.

Chapter Three

Susan woke up and heard snoring beside her. She stiffened, confusion etched on her face. Did she have sex? She removed her covers and saw she was fully dressed. She breathed a sigh of relief.

She turned to glance at Jack as he slept. There was something about him, she felt almost protective of him. She took in his chiseled black face, strong jawline. *Damn what was she thinking.*

She heard knocking on her door and froze. *What were they going to think?*

Jack woke, glanced at her and his eyes widened, "Did we have sex?" He said it as if he had bitten into a rotten fruit. Susan wanted to comment but the knocking came again.

She snorted instead, "in your dreams. Get out of my bed."

Susan went to the door, tying a scarf over her head. She opened the door and stared at the smug face of Joseph Muku, their local guide. He was wearing a sleeveless shirt, buttons opened showing his abs.

"We're leaving for the caves and I ah—" He paused as Jack poked his head, "oh I see, the deed has been done."

Susan snorted, rolling her eyes. "You've such a vivid imagination." She grabbed Jack by the elbows and shoved him out of her room. "Your boy slept like a baby."

"Ooh!!" Muku said as he began to laugh.

Jack scowled at Susan. "You're like a sister to me."

Susan arched an eyebrow and raised a finger silencing them both. "Don't you have a tour to plan?" She tilted her head at the two guys.

Muku stuttered and said, "of course, Mademoiselle."

It was now the turn of Jack to chuckle as Muku shook his head his head and elbowed Jack on his way.

Jack turned to Susan to say something but the look on her face was enough to silence him. She stared at his shoulders as he walked away. She knew she had probably hurt his feelings, but she was confused about him. *Why did he sometimes treat her like she was his sister?*

She closed her door and got ready for the tour.

"COME ON," SAID MUKU, hands on hips as he chuckled. "Young people of now have no desire for exercise and yet want to go on a tour to the famous Mount Elgon, huh?"

Professor Jones Harrison snorted as he adjusted his glasses. "And I suppose you don't even break a sweat?" he said each word punctuated by a breath. "That's why the treadmill was invented young man."

Muku chuckled and shook his head. "We're almost at the mouth of the caves." He said then scowled. "Where some kids said they saw some ghost warrior."

Behind the professor, Susan was sweating profusely, she kept slapping mosquitoes.

"Here take this," said Jack, handing her an ointment.

Susan murmured saying her thanks.

Further behind, Chloe and Mark were taking selfies. Joana the model was posing for her camera man as she sometimes shot Jack a sultry look. Susan pretended not to notice but she was not going to fall for that. For some reason Jack seemed to reciprocate the model's advances. She knew he was probably getting back at her for humiliating him.

"Ah finally," shouted Muku as he neared an ancient cave.

Jones took of his hat. "It looks quite preserved. Africans sometimes don't value these historical sites."

"This will be perfect!" Joana said as she stood before the mouth of the cave and arched her back, posing for the camera. She licked her lips as she stared at Jack. Susan saw their interaction.

Muku's eye met Susan and seemed to say I told you so. She felt blood rush to her face as her pulse pounded in her ears.

Boys will always be boys, she thought. She saw the sympathy in Muku's eyes and looked away. She wasn't some broken thing to be comforted. Jones was still admiring the mouth of the cave, commenting on the pristine nature of the cave.

As for Chloe and Mark, they stole kisses when the professor wasn't looking. She envied them.

"Mark over here!" Jones said as Mark broke away from Chloe and rushed forward. "Record this."

Susan stood aside as Jones began to talk about the cave and its discovery. Her mind wandered to her late mother and some of the strange things she had said to her before she had died.

The professor had allowed her on the trip partly because she had let it slip about her Ugandan heritage. There was a reason why her name had two initials. She had been crying when her mother had told her about their heritage on her deathbed. She snapped from her thoughts as Muku said something about them entering the cave with their lights. A twig snapped on her right and she turned her heard and screamed when a strangely dressed woman rushed at her and grabbed her hands. Susan froze as the woman began to speak to her in Swahili. Jack was the first to pull her away, her face full of terror.

"What was that?" Susan said, heart pounding in her chest as she struggled to breath.

"That was interesting," Jones said, shaken but attempting to sound nonchalant. Everyone was quiet, shaken at the strange turn of events. "My Swahili is rusty. What at all did she mean?"

Susan turned to Muku and stiffened when she saw the look on his face. It was like a man who had seen a ghost. "Joseph?"

Muku shook his head making a sign of the cross.

"What did she mean?" Jack asked, rubbing the shoulders of Susan.

Muku inhaled, expelling a breath, "she said Ndembe will meet the past." He stared hard at Susan whose face had gone blank.

"What does it mean—" Jack asked, his stare shifting between Susan and Joseph.

Muku pursed his lips, glanced at Susan and shrugged. "We need to get inside the cave. The sun will go down very soon." But not before Susan saw the stare from him. *We will need to talk about this.*

"All this drama just makes me want to enter the cave," Joana said, pointing at the cave with a manicured finger.

"Shall we?" Jones said as he glanced at Muku who nodded.

The group filed in to the cave, their high beam torches illuminating the walls of the cave. They all paused, transfixed by what they were seeing.

"What the hell?" Joseph Muku said as he stiffened, terror on his face.

Chapter Four

The group stared in shock at the sketches on the walls of the cave.

"This is impossible," said Muku as a scowl deepened on his face. "These sketches were not here the last time I was here."

Jones frowned, glancing between the sketches on the walls of the cave and their local guide. "You're sure you didn't have too much to drink?"

The comment drew a chuckle from the group.

Muku shook his head and opened his mouth to retort when Jones raised his hand. "Chloe, get over here."

Chloe donning her spectacles, joined the professor, "do you think these sketches were drawn recently?"

Cloe bent down, illuminating the walls once again with her torch. She bit her lip in concentration. "These sketches are old."

Muku shook his head. "I know what I saw, and these sketches were not here." He noted Susan had gone deathly quiet, clutching something around her neck. "Are you okay?" She nodded as he saw Jack giving him a hard stare.

Jones edged closer to the sketches and frowned, "interesting how whoever sketched this was trying to tell a story. The Bunyoro Kitara history has been very elusive to us historians."

"I thought the Bunyoro Kitara was a myth?" Mark said as he had been very reserved all this while.

At the mouth of the cave Joana had refused to enter after seeing the sketches.

"The Bunyoro were real. You may have heard of the Bacchwesi or Chwezi. Though the history of the Bunyoro is steeped in myth. The empire of Kitara tells the history of a warrior like people." Jones flashed his torch at the sketches as he began to move deeper into the cave. "These sketches tell the history of a princess. This is strange."

The cave tapered to a dead end. "I thought the cave went on further," Jack said as he turned to give a hard stare to their guide. "Are you sure you brought us to the right cave?"

"Are you trying to tell me how to do my job?" Muku said testily as he shoved past Jack. "This cave should have gone on further. This is new and I don't like this."

Susan had been withdrawn throughout the journey in the cave. The sketches were reminding her of the things her mother had said. She had thought it was the ramblings of a dying woman. She tightened her hand around the amulet hanging around her neck. She felt the eyes of Muku on her and saw the concern in his gaze. Jack frowned when he saw the glances between them but said nothing.

Jack got close to the professor, and they began to have an animated conversation. Behind her, Chloe and Mark stood close to each other taking solace in their proximity.

"You seem lost in your thoughts?" Muku said, pressing for a response from her.

Susan simply smiled, fingering the amulet. She frowned when she saw Jack point out something at the dead end of the cave and glanced at her.

"Okay, that's strange," said Muku, "doesn't it seem weird that Jack and Prof. are both looking at you?"

Susan frowned. She noticed the professor signaling her to come forward. She approached them apprehensively with Muku shadowing her.

"Can I have your amulet?" said Jack as a frown deepened on Susan's face. Confusion etched on her face. Behind her the rest of the group were perplexed as well.

"Ah, what's going on here?" Muku asked, glancing suspiciously at Jack and the professor. The professor seemed to see Jack for the first time.

Susan hesitated. "Please?" Jack's eyes seemed to plead. She finally relented and handed it over. Jack took the amulet and placed it inside a cleft in the wall.

"How did that get there?" Muku said, an even deeper frown on his face.

"I always knew your heritage would come in handy one day," Jones said.

"You know this is where something bad happens when you twist the amulet right?" Muku said with a tight smile. "And why is an amulet from Susan fitting into that cleft?"

"It's complicated," Susan replied.

"I don't think we should go down the rabbit hole," Muku said, "I believe the kids saw something terrible."

"Old wives' tale," said Jack. "I thought Ugandan men were brave. I was wrong."

Muku swore, eyes hardening. "You're so full of shi—"

"Enough! This is a historic find. You have no idea the years I have spent on this." Jones said, his speech silencing them. He nodded to Jack to go ahead.

"Here goes nothing," Jack said as he twisted the amulet clockwise in the cleft. They all waited with bated breath.

"Phew!" Muku clicked his tongue, "well I—"

A grating sound was heard as if gears were moving beneath them, and the ground under their feet caved in. They plunged downwards, their screams reverberating around them as they fell into a pool of water.

Susan gasped for breath as she resurfaced and heard a whimper. "What just happ—" She turned and screamed when she saw the caricature of a tall man, face painted, body sculpted like a god with a loin cloth around his waist as he levelled a spear against them. More of them began to surround them. Stalactites above them illuminated the cave they had fallen into.

"Oh shit!" Muku said when he spied the strangers.

"The Bacchwesi!" Jones whispered, almost reverently.

Then a shot rang out and one of the warriors fell.

"Noo!" Muku shouted as chaos broke out. Mark had a pistol in his hands and was firing off rounds as Chloe covered her ears, screaming. Susan couldn't breathe as she saw a warrior heft a spear and threw it as it impaled Mark in the chest, the pistol falling from his grasp.

Muku shouted in a language and the warriors stilled. One of them came forward, spat, and levelled his spear against them. Susan stiffened but said nothing.

"What are they saying?" Jack said, simmering aggression in his eyes.

"We have to go with them if we are to survive." Muku said.

Susan put an arm around Chloe who was sobbing and hyperventilating. She glared at the strangers and the professor who seemed to be in awe of them.

The warriors led them out of the pool and towards an opening in the cave as sunlight hit them in their faces, blinding them.

"What the—" Muku said and paused, mouth opened in shock.

Jack's lips were pursed as he glanced around, rage in them. Susan saw it and prayed he wouldn't do anything foolish to get himself killed. The group stared in bewilderment at the mouth of the cave from which they had emerged.

"The Bunyoro are still alive. How incredible!" Jones said, "This will change our entire perception on the history of Kitara. I wonder where we are. Some said they were aliens. Some said—"

Susan stared hard at the professor. "Mark is dead and the only thing you care about is some long-forgotten history and your fame?"

Jones stared back at her and seemed to come to his senses. "I'm—"

Susan raised a hand, "You're a jerk, you know that right?" Jones paused shock on his face. "Always wanted to say that to your face."

Jones was about to retort when a warrior poked his back with a spear. They group crested a hill and came to stand still, awe and shock on their faces as they gazed at the settlement before them.

"Holy shit!" Muku whispered.

Chapter Five

"You must remember your roots, Nyinamwiru." Susan stared at her withered mother as she clasped her hand. "You must never forget who you are. One day your past will come calling and you must heed the call, my daughter."

Memories assailed her as she stared upon the settlements before them.

"This is impossible," Muku said beside her as they were herded by the warriors behind them. Around them, the strangers eyed them suspiciously.

Women with their faces painted, midriff bare hid their children behind them. Susan felt her heart thumping even as she held Chloe who was still whimpering from the death of Mark. This was a dream, her mind was telling her. Yet here they were, a whole civilization from the past was here. *How was this possible?* She had read Jules Verne as a kid and yet this was surreal. *How could an entire civilization be sequestered away from the world like that?* In front of her Jones was still in awe. He couldn't help but make comments about the historical inaccuracies in the myths of the Bacchwesi. Beside the professor, Jack had gone quiet. Susan felt a foreboding in her gut. Jack's demeanor had changed once they had come out of the cave. Everything about his body language was like a cheetah ready to spring upon its prey.

Directly in front of them was a huge wooden pavilion. Susan glanced back. Mount Elgon was behind them. She reached for the amulet around her neck and paused when she realized it wasn't there. They were ushered into the pavilion where they came face to face with the king, a descendant it seemed.

Spears at their back prodded them to kneel. Warriors lined the way to the king who was dressed in his battle like regalia with a skull hanging around his neck. His face was painted, giving him the look of one who was perpetually awake.

One of the warriors stepped forward and said something to the king who stiffened slightly when a warrior pulled out Susan's amulet.

"What are they saying?" Jones whispered.

Muku swallowed, looked around fearfully as his eyes met Susan, "they are looking for the owner of the amulet?"

Jack swore as his eyes met that of Susan.

"I knew Susan's heritage had something to do with the Bacchwesi but I didn't know it would be this big." Jones whispered.

Jack hissed at the professor who arched an eyebrow as the warriors glanced at them at the mention of Bacchwesi. "Is that Bantu they are speaking?"

Muku nodded and glanced suspiciously at Jack. He kept glancing at Susan, a questioning look on his face. The warrior who had the amulet was still in deep conversation with the king. The king said a name 'Nyinamwiru' and there was a collective gasp.

Susan felt her ears pounding as her heart was thumping in her chest. Her throat felt dry as the king's eyes settled on them.

"What's happening?" Chloe asked, her voice hoarse from crying.

Professor Jones Harrison's eyes widened as he glanced at Susan, shock on his face. "You are a descendant." He whispered, awe on his face.

Both Muku and Chloe could only stare in shock at Susan who couldn't look them in the face.

"Oh no! They will kill you if they find out."

The lead warrior levelled his spear at Muku and said some harsh words in old Bantu.

"Tell them it's me." Jack said to Muku who shook his head.

"No!"

The warrior said something to Muku who stiffened. "The king is a descendant of Bukuku."

Jones swore, a helpless look on his face. "They will kill her if they find out."

"To hell with this," Jack sprung up, putting the warriors on alert. "Tell him I challenge him." Muku translated his request.

The king said something in Bantu and Jack glanced towards Muku. "He has accepted your duel." Muku said, glancing fearfully at Jack, a newfound respect in his eyes for him. "It is a fight to the death."

Jack stiffened and raised his chin, staring defiantly at the king. "I accept." The warriors tapped the butt of their spears on the ground.

Jones ruffled his hair. "This is a bad dream."

The chief warrior spoke rapidly in Bantu, and they were led out from the pavilion into a wooden structure where they were locked up.

Susan approached Jack, confusion etched on her face. "That was very stupid of you to do." She said, tears stinging her eyes. "You didn't have to do that."

"You forget that a gentleman must always save the damsel."

Around them the group had gone silent.

"This is not a game, Jack." Susan said, "you could die."

Jack stepped back and leaned against the wooden prison. He closed his eyes. "There was no other choice and how in the name of God does Joseph understand Bantu? I thought the language was dead."

Susan stared hard at Jack. She knew he was trying to deflect her questions.

Muku shrugged. "The Bacchwesi were our ancestors, plus I took some courses in the dead languages."

Jones had been very quiet, a frown on his face. He turned to Susan. "The name the king mentioned 'Nyinamwiru?'" He glanced questioningly at Susan who shrank under his gaze.

Susan exhaled. "My full name is Susan Ndembe Nyinamwiru Williams."

Muku whistled as Chloe's face went blank. The professor passed a hand across his face unbuttoning the collar of his shirt.

"They will kill all of us if they realise Jack is lying to them and that you are the real descendant." Jones said.

"What's the deal with her name anyway?" Chloe said, tears in her eyes. "Mark didn't have to die."

"Mark died because the warriors acted in self-defense." Jack replied as Chloe burst into fresh tears.

Susan shot him a withering look as he clammed up. Muku glanced at Susan and licked his lips. "Tell me more about your roots. Maybe I might glean something from it to bargain our way out of here." Susan closed her eyes, bracing herself to release a burden she had kept for so long. "My mother like her mother before her, passed on the tradition to me. I know most of you have heard of the myth of Nyinamwiru. I will let Prof tell you of the myth and I will take it from there."

Outside the sun was setting and they could hear drums. Susan saw a strange look in Jack's face but pinned it down to their circumstance. *Were they in a different dimension?*

Professor Jones Harrison fingered his salt and pepper beard. "The story goes that when the Bacchwesi founded the Bunyoro kingdom, there were led by a king called Bukuku. He wanted to rule forever on the throne so when he was told that his daughter Nyinamwiru would birth a boy that would dethrone him, he became furious and fearful, and plotted ways to have her killed."

"Isn't that the story of every king?" Chloe interjected.

Jones smiled. "But fate smiled on Nyinamwiru as the king was advised against killing her daughter. Legend says she became pregnant and escaped from the palace. History doesn't really tell us much about what really happened. In some versions a god sneaks her out."

They all looked to Susan who had pursed her lips.

"Well, the myths was right on one thing. Nyinamwiru did give birth but knowing that her father would kill her child connived with her maids and a trusted friend Lumumba, a clay potter. He was entrusted with the child and now you know the end of the story."

"Sad thing the world will never get to hear of this," said Muku, a sullen look on his face.

Chloe sobbed, "I don't want to die in this shithole."

"We all agree on that. None of you will die here." Jack said with certainty, surprising all of them. The comment brought fresh tears to Susan's eyes.

"But why?" Chloe asked as they all turned to her. "It's not like Susan wants the throne, right?"

They all looked towards Susan who shrugged. "I have lived my entire life with this cursed knowledge. I can't let Jack die in my place."

Jack snarled. "You're crazy. You can't go up against the king. You are not ready yet."

Susan frowned, confused at his statement, "What do you—all of sudden you want to die for me?"

"You don't understand. It is my—"

"Enough!" Jones said shocking all of them, "Joe, is there anything we can do to get out of this?"

Muku contemplated the question. "Unless Susan reveals who she is."

Footsteps approached their cell, and the gates were unlocked. They were herded out of the cell. Outside the night sky was clear. *How far back in the past were they or were they in a different dimension?* Susan contemplated as they headed towards a spot. The Bacchwesi had formed a ring. Two spears were stuck into the ground. The lead warrior stood by one of the spears directly facing them. He was naked save a cloth covering his loins. His muscles rippled across his chest. Jack went to stand by the second spear, his back to the group. Susan felt her heart hammering in her chest. Behind the lead warrior, the king sat there stoic, surrounded by his warriors.

Jack removed his top, muscles bunching together as he flexed them. The drums which had been playing stilled. The fire played across his features as he turned to face the group, a similar amulet hanging around his neck. Susan frowned. Jones and Muku swore. Jack bowed his head to Susan and nodded at her as her eyes stinged with tears.

"I don't understand," Susan said, hand to her mouth as her emotions overwhelmed her.

"This changes things," Muku said, "your boyfriend has his own skeletons in his closet."

Susan shot Jones a hard look, "I didn't know, I swear to God."

"Well, it seems you have a guardian after all." Joseph Muku said as Jack gripped his spear.

Jack levelled his spear at the warrior and spoke in Bantu and turned sideways to address Susan.

"Oh no!" Susan said, choking on her tears as trepidation crawled up her spine.

The warrior facing Jack stiffened and turned to his king who had a furious scowl oh his face. His eyes blazed with fury. Around them the crowd had began to murmur. The lead warrior gripped his spear and bowed to Jack.

Jack did same and raised his spear and shouted, "To Nyinamwiru!"

The combatants circled each other, gauging each other's weakness, the drums rising in tempo and the warriors circled each other like two lions and then they rushed at each other. The Professor and his group gazed on, their heart in their throats.

Chapter Six.

The man called Jack Quainoo also known in his past life as Isimbwa the hunter gripped the spear in his hand. Around him, the drums were being played. For centuries he had waited to get his revenge. Each time when he was close to finding the doorway, it eluded him. Behind him, he saw the shock on Susan's face. It was unfortunate he had to lie to her. She wouldn't have believed him if he had told her his identity.

Jack snapped his mind to the present as the chief warrior rushed him, but he sidestepped him easily as he parried his thrust. They began a dance of death as he lunged and was blocked. A parry here, a feint and the duel had began in earnest. Their bodies were slick with sweat.

He saw the pensive look on the faces of his colleagues. He needed to end this. The chief warrior rushed at him, murder in his eyes. That was a mistake. Jack parried the blow and used the warrior's momentum against him as he flung the warrior to the ground on his head, snapping his head. The crack reverberated across the open ground. The drums and chanting stopped, the entire area had gone silent.

Jack raised his eyes to meet the king. Their eyes met and in that instant Jack knew his old enemy still lurked in there. The king's eyes widened as recognition flashed in his eyes. He opened his mouth to shout a command but Jack was faster as the memories of Isimbwa the hunter flashed through his mind. He shouted "Isimbwa!" and gripped the spear, hefted it even as the warriors reacted too late. He threw it with all his strength as it impaled the reincarnation of King Bukuku in his chest, blood gurgling from his mouth. There was sudden quiet as the shock of the Bacchwesi at seeing their king dead.

Jack turned to stare at Susan and the professor as he nodded at them, his face grim.

"Run!" then the wailing began as the warriors rushed at Jack.

Joseph Muku didn't need to be told twice as she grabbed Susan and Chloe. "Let's go," he screamed as chaos broke out. It seemed the Bacchwesi had broken into two factions. Some chanting the name of

Isimbwa the hunter and Nyinamwiru as they clashed with warriors of the dead king Bukuku. In the chaos, Professor Jones and his team slipped unnoticed as battle raged.

They went a little further and Susan turned. "We can't leave him there." She said, tears running down her face. Jack was standing his ground, yet she knew he was being overwhelmed. He was bleeding from several places on his body.

"There is nothing you can do," Jones said, his face drawn tight with fear.

"I don't want to die here," Chloe said, sobbing as she gripped Muku's hand. A few meters from them they could see the screams of the dying and the fighters.

Susan straightened as she closed her eyes and took a deep breath. Her mother's dying words came back to her. "Can you speak Bantu fluently?" she said, staring hard at Muku.

He nodded his head, a scowl on his face. "This is a very bad idea."

"Susan," Jones admonished. "I understand how you feel."

Susan whirled on the Professor, eyes blazing. "You don't know how I feel," she seethed. "You've no idea!"

"Muku!" Susan said as she broke away from her colleagues and sauntered towards the chaos, shoulders held high. "Translate what I say."

"I'm Susan Nyinamwiru Ndembe Williams, descendant of Queen Nyinamwiru, daughter of King Bukuku." She said as the fighting stopped and a heavy silence descended on them as Susan walked through them. She began to walk towards Jack who was kneeling, leaning on his spear. Her heart broke when she saw him.

Jack saw the questions in her descendant's eyes. His breath wheezed as he stretched forth his hand and Susan grabbed it. She didn't need to ask any questions but felt the unadulterated love from her father if she could call him that.

"Nyinamwiru, Sun of my world." Jack said as he took his last breath as a sigh escaped him. Behind her, Susan heard Chloe sobbing uncontrollably. Susan took a deep breath. Her gaze scanned around at her people. No matter the crime committed against her ancestors, it had to end.

"There lies Isimbwa, great hunter and husband to Queen Nyinamwiru. Honour him." Beside her Muku translated in Bantu. Jones and Chloe had crept closer. Susan walked towards the throne, and nobody dared stopped her. The king's body lay slumped before the throne. She stood before the throne as the weight of her ancestry bore down on her. It was time for the sins of the past to be corrected once and for all. She stripped the dead king of her amulet and held it in her hands. It began to glow. At last, the heir to the Bacchwesi had come as the prophecy foretold.

Before her there was awe on the faces of the Bacchwesi. The people began to bow as they began to chant her name.

"Nyinamwiru!

"Nyinamwiru!"

"Nyinamwiru!"

Professor Jones grinned and shouted, "long live the Empire of Kitara. Long live the Bacchwesi!."

Epilogue

"Well, I'm certainly going to miss this place." Professor Jones said as held his hat in his hand and gazed across the settlement of the Bacchwesi. "A pity no one will ever believe that."

Chloe snorted and shook her head. "Can we get out of here before they change their minds."

Susan chuckled as she put an arm around Chloe.

"You could have stayed," Muku said as she stared at Susan in the eye as she blushed. "You could have become queen and I would have been your consort."

They all chuckled as they made their way back towards the Mount Elgon. After the fighting and the burial of Isimbwa known to them as Jack Quainoo, the team had learnt that when Isimbwa had learnt that Nyinamwiru had been killed after her child had been spirited away. He had invoked a curse on the Bacchwesi and that their spirits would never rest once he hadn't taken his revenge. Behind the group the rest of the Bacchwesi had lined up to see them off.

The team entered the cave where they had fallen into the pool and paused when they didn't see the body of Mark. Muku was going to remark on it when a hard stare by Susan stopped him. They headed towards a section of the wall where they had been told to insert the two amulets. Susan inserted the amulets and the wall slid away to reveal the path to the cave they had entered earlier. They saw a body lying on the ground and Chloe rushed towards it and screamed.

They were frozen as Mark woke up and touch his chest and head. "I just had the weirdest dream."

Chloe hugged him and began to fuss over him. "You're alive."

"Of course, I'm alive but I don't understand I had the weirdest dream that someone was pulling me from some pool and that I didn't belong in this time—"

Susan choked and Mark stared at her strangely.

"Well, we have had a very long day and we all need some rest." Jones winked at the group. "Must have been the air in the cave. Maybe we passed out." He said as he stared hard at each member to refute his story. No one did.

Susan turned to stare at where they had come from but all she saw was an image of a hunter bowing to a woman with two amulets around her neck. "How did it get there?"

Muku came to stand close to her and chuckled. He looked towards the image on the wall and stared at Susan.

"What?"

"You still don't see it. Look at the image of the woman well."

Susan stared hard at the image of the woman on the wall and a coy smile played on her lips. "I guess no one will ever know."

"Maybe we can change that"

"How?"

"We can tell their story. How one woman, Nyinamwiru's bravery saved her people." Muku said this while gazing deep into Susan's eye. The kiss when it happened was short and deep.

Susan playfully pushed him away, her hand lingering on his chest. "Well, I don't think we can write the story of Nyinamwiru under these conditions." She said biting her lips as Muku laughed.

"Are you guys coming or not?" Jones shouted back there, eliciting giggles from Mark and Chloe.

"Take the lead I will follow."

Susan Nyinamwiru Ndembe Williams stood under the sketch of her great ancestor Isimbwa and clutched the two amulets around her neck. Strange that the group had not mentioned Jack, but she was the only one who remembered him. Maybe it was part of the curse being lifted. He would be forgotten.

She placed her hand on the sketch of the woman with similar amulets around her neck. She knew who it was now.

"Long live the Bacchwesi. Long Live Nyinamwiru!"

The End

BONUS STORY
FIRST CONTACT

CHAPTER ONE

The first time the ship entered earth's atmosphere, Greg Wilson, newly recruited into NASA, was dozing off at his console. The first time he got recruited into NASA, it had felt like a dream come true. Two years working at the observatory had taught him about the drab nature of the job. So when the alarms started going off, he awoke suddenly, hand hitting his coffee cup as its contents spilled on his board.

"Shit!"

He glanced at the readings on the screen as the beeping continued. The hair on his nape stiffened and goose pimples spread all over his body.

"What the–"

Eyes wide, Greg did a double take, wiped the drool from his mouth and stared at the screen again, blinking rapidly. He made a print out, grabbed it and stared at it to be sure he wasn't hallucinating. He dialed a number on his landline.

"Dave, you've got to see this," Greg continued to stare at the screen and at the report he held in his hand. A heavy set man with salt and pepper hair came towards him, a furious scowl on his face.

"This better be good, lad." David Pence said as he took the printout from Greg's outstretched hand.

Dave stared at the report and then at the screen. "Is this authentic?"

Greg only nodded. Some colleagues had began to gather around the observatory, mumbling undertone at the discovery.

"What happens now" asked Greg, looking up to his supervisor for answers.

David Pence sighed. Never in his ten years as a NASA scientist did he envision that a day like this would come. David studied the screen and asked, "Based on its current trajectory, where is it headed?"

Greg typed commands into his keyboard as he waited for his extrapolation. An intake of breath sounded from someone behind him. There were murmurs across the room. A faint beeping sound could still be heard.

"Antarctica," Greg said, scowling at what that meant. "Why Antarctica?"

Everyone in the room was excited. A discovery like this would mean a great deal for NASA.

Dave turned to his employees as they eagerly awaited what to do next.

"Gentlemen," his sharp eyes roamed over them, settling on Greg. "Let's find where this ship comes from."

People scrambled to their stations as men and women jostled each other to map out the origins of the mysterious ship. Greg and Dave were left alone, each contemplating what this discovery meant to the wider world.

"Do you think it's alien?" asked Greg, his voice hopeful.

"Let's just hope it's just E.T coming to pay us a visit in peace then."

CHAPTER TWO

The headquarters of Africanus was a beehive of activity as the chopper carrying the commander-in-chief of the Black Federation swooped towards the helipad. Government officials were scuffling about in a frenzied hurry to get to the crisis room for the impending meeting. The chopper landed on the helipad and a slender man slipped out followed by his guards. Matthew Assan, a former citizen of the then West African country, Ghana, shook the hands of his aide.

"What's the update?" he asked the aide as he was led to the crisis room. A hundred years after the Doomsday Attack, the African nations had come together under the name Africanus and the Black Federation was the standing army of the united countries. The African union had been disbanded years earlier for its ineffectiveness in achieving the aims it had set out to achieve. Some said the integration of the African nations had been inevitable following the D-day attack. Some said the North Koreans had started it. Others said the irrevocable act by a certain Western leader had plunged the world into a devastating war which had nearly wiped out the human race.

"The ship is headed towards Antarctica." Paul Nketchi said, consulting his phone for updates. Matthew grimaced as they entered the crisis room. The individuals in the room stood up. He inclined his head and took his seat at the head of U-shaped mahogany table. Around them various large screen monitors displayed various activities across all the African states and the wider world as well.

Paul Nketchi, fumbling with his suitcase took out a paper and placed it in front of the commander.

"What is the status?" Matthew asked in a sharp voice. Each member state of Africanus had their military general in the room. Matthew was the head.

"Our contacts with our mutual friends indicate they have no idea about the ship and how it entered the earth's atmosphere. They are equally stumped as we are." Brian Adamu, a Kenyan general said.

Matthew sighed, "We must find out if this ship poses a threat." He paused when someone cleared his throat. All eyes turned to Peter Ndochie, one of the oldest and experienced veterans on the command.

"If our partners say this ship is not theirs, might we not entertain the possibility of what we're all thinking but do not want to say."

The command center was silent.

Matthew leaned forward, glancing briefly at his aide, Paul who mouthed "I told you so."

"General Ndochie, please explain." He asked, an eyebrow raised.

Peter Ndochie sat straight. "The talk on the network is this could be it," he paused as he licked his lips.

A glance around the command center showed the uneasiness of where the conversation was leading to. Nobody needed to spit it out. For years after the atomic war, nations had been hesitant to denuclearize. Africa had not being the target yet it had been affected. The devastations caused by the nuclear weapons had been catastrophic. No continent had been left intact. Even after a hundred years, famine, and radiation poisoning were killing off many people. It was almost like the earth was dying. How nuclear weapons could have gone rogue was something that couldn't be explained? London, New York, Kremlin, India and China had been the hardest hit. No one had seen it coming. In one single day, more than a billion people had been killed. Some said it was the work of a clandestine extinction seekers but no evidence had been found out. After the D-day attack, nations had gone to war against each other. That had been the worst mistake of the century. More than half the population on earth had been obliterated in a single week from rogue nuclear weapons.

"It could be an alien invasion." The General said as Matthew whipped his head around, pulling him from the past.

Murmurs and bursts of laughter echoed across the room. Matthew raised an arm as the room fell silent.

"We must assess this risk." He said, eyes roaming around his fellow Africanus brothers. "We don't want a repeat of the D-day."

Every single person nodded. They were all too aware of what their commander-in-chief meant by the D-day. All of them had not being born but they were experiencing the aftermath.

"What now?" William Mandela, a descendant of the Mandela bloodline said.

Everyone stared at Matthew waiting for his decision. No one wanted another war but the Africanus had learnt their lesson.

"We go to Antarctica."

CHAPTER THREE

The Pentagon or what was left of it after the D-day attack was a flurry of activity as Laura Henderson; Secretary of Defense took her seat in the briefing room. Before her were all the heads of the security agencies in the United States. Around them, pictures of the former heads of the security were framed. How did we get here? Laura thought to herself.

Around the table, everyone had been given a photo of the ship's first entry into the earth's atmosphere. A high resolution image would be presented to them by NASA.

Laura glanced at the shot, pulled her spectacles to the bridge of her nose and looked towards the gentlemen in the room. A hundred years after the D-day and still it was a problem for a woman to head anything.

"Gentlemen, we have a crisis on our hands. NASA has confirmed these images. Subject has landed at Antarctica as we speak. Any news from the other side?" Laura said, staring at the men before her.

William Hobbs, director of the CIA cleared his throat, "Our sources seem to suggest the ship did not come from them." The other heads of security also nodded their heads to this bit of information.

"And this has been verified?"

Hobbs nodded as the room descended into an uncomfortable silence. The secretary of defense took off her glasses. "Are we talking about an invasion?" said Laura, eyes roaming around the room. "We need more than just guesswork. Has NASA come through with the possible origins?"

"We may have to consider every option, Madam Secretary," said George Hitchens, director of Homeland Security. "But we also need to consider this might be a ploy from somewhere to get our guard down and then they will strike again."

Around the room, heads nodded. Ever since the D-day attack, all nations had been on alert. The African nations had banded together at last. Even the Islamic countries had come together, something unheard off. The threat of another war had been imminent, it hang in the air, pulsing its final breath. The appearance of the ship had escalated the tensions.

Laura Henderson knew all too well what was facing her. The president wanted options and answers. Any misstep and the world would be plunged into another nuclear war. A hundred years ago, after the D-day attack, a certain president had made a decision which had nearly plunged the world into extinction. A nuclear weapon had been unleashed on the East. The consequences had been grave. The retaliation had been swift. Different bombings taking place across the US had crippled the greatest economy in the world. Laura knew only one option was available. They had to get to Antarctica first.

CHAPTER FOUR

Dimitri Nicholav stared at his family as they celebrated his fiftieth birthday. It was a wonder they could even celebrate a birthday with the gloom over the country. No one had been spared in the D-day attack. Why didn't anyone see it coming? For such an audacious plan to have been effected it needed massive funding and infrastructure. History was never the same after the attack. Dimitri Nicholav's grandfather was at the Kremlin when the attack happened. How it was synchronized to happen simultaneously around the world was still a mystery to all the security agencies? His grandfather had died protecting the president. Before the D-day attack, Russia was becoming what it was once again, a nation not to be trifled with. And now staring at his family, such a moment was so rare it was to be cherished.

He saw Banachek approaching him, his face grim. He whispered something into his ear and Dimitri stiffened.

"Impossible!" he said in his gruff voice as he stood up. His family was surprised. "Go to go, Mama."

Dimitri kissed his mother's forehead, bid his family farewell and was ushered into a black convoy back to the Kremlin. He closed his eyes, face becoming stoic at the implications of what he was about to do. The world was dying. Tensions had been rising in the Middle East ever since the D-day attack. Sources said an imminent attack was probable and now this ship. Even as the convoy sped towards the Kremlin, horns and sirens blaring as cars made way for the prime minister. Dimitri's mind wandered to the distant past. After Putin's change in the constitution decades ago, the prime minister had become the most powerful person in Russia, not even the president had that much power. Yet everything had come crushing down after that. Russia, a formidable superpower had suffered such devastating attack that it had never recovered from.

Dimitri sighed, relegating the morbid thoughts to the recesses of his mind. The once magnificent Kremlin was a pale comparison to its former glory. Dimitri stared at the images of the ship before him. He didn't believe in extraterrestrial life yet he could not help but wonder where the ship had come from. Even the United States was confounded as well, his sources revealed. Everyone was on high alert, no one wanted to be caught unawares. The report said the ship's trajectory was towards Antarctica. Why would it land there? Dimitri knew whatever the ship was, they had to get there first.

CHAPTER FIVE

The seal nuzzled its mother as they lay on a thin scrap of ice in Antarctica. If it had any superior intelligence, it would have been conscious of the scraps of ice left. Antarctica was melting at an astronomical rate. Most of it was covered in water. The polar bears were extinct. They weren't the only ones. The baby seal did not know this as it attempted to flip onto its back. The two were the last of their kind. Its mother heard a whirring sound and perked up, whiskers twitching as it trembled. They stared at the ship which flew over them. They scrambled from their thin scrap of ice and dived into the ice cold waters.

The ship glided over the water, wobbling a bit but straightening as it made for a patch of land. It slowed down as metal legs extended underneath it as it landed, a hissing sound emanating from it. A whirring sound was heard as a blue shield encompassed it. It stood there waiting as it emitted a rather strange beeping sound.

CHAPTER SIX

The supreme leader of Iran sat cross legged in his room, as he meditated. Whenever he retired to this solitary confinement, no one dared disturb his solitude or risk severe punishment. He tried not to think of the several decades of unrest caused by the D-day attack. A lot of people thought the attack originated from them, far from it, they had been equally astounded as them. They had been attacked as well. Years before President Trump had assassinated their topmost general, their retaliation had been minimal and the world thought it was over but they had been planning in secret. When the D-day attack happened, the West had blamed them and had unleashed a nuclear weapon on them. They had seen it coming and had prepared for it. Long before the D-day attack happened, they had been bidding their time. But something unprecedented had happened. When the Americans unleashed their arsenal of weapons against the East, the weapons had been redirected towards unintended targets. The world was in an uproar as each retaliated and a nuclear wipeout of the human race had nearly occurred. By the time the mistake was realized, it had become too late. But the damage had been done, trust broken, whole cities destroyed and millions of people annihilated. Whoever had engineered the D-day attack had extrapolated such intended consequences. But they probably didn't envision the East banding together. The supreme leader's musings were cut short by a rapid knocking on his door. He frowned as someone opened his door and a turban appeared followed by the face of his most trusted bodyguard. He glared at him, yet the look on his face made him pause.

He silently followed his bodyguard into a secure room where monitors were displaying real time news. His bodyguard pointed towards a screen showing a grainy footage of a ship. The supreme leader turned to the people in the room to seek for confirmation. Their grim faces told him everything. He approached a black landline and initiated a call. It was time his Muslim brothers redeemed the pledges they made after the D-day attacks. It was time to show the West a new superpower. Antarctica was no man's land and whatever was waiting there, they would get to it first.

CHAPTER SEVEN

Arjun Singh tightened his fist as he stared at the room full of generals from different parts of India. Around the briefing room, aides shuffled back and forth as papers were distributed among the generals. A bead of sweat run down his cheek. His turban felt hot and stuffy on his head and yet he couldn't show weakness in front of the generals. His gaze settled upon one general who nodded, a Muslim. The D-day attack like most countries had nearly wiped out three quarters of India's population. Since then the deeply entrenched caste system in the country had been abolished. Unity had been forged even as the country was still reeling from shock. Arjun Singh, a minority was now the prime minister, something unthinkable a century ago. He had read about the legacy of Narendra Modi. He had done a great job but had exacerbated the caste system with his citizenship registration. The nation had been deeply divided even before the D-day attack. Arjun tapped his microphone to alert the generals for the meeting to begin.

"Gentlemen, we need to make a decision about this," said Arjun referring to the image before him. He didn't want to call it alien. He was a devout Muslim. His religion left no space for him to believe in such nonsense of any kind yet the mysterious ship was a puzzle to everyone. Tensions were already rising around the world.

Someone cleared his throat. Arjun nodded his head towards the minister for security, Ganesh.

"I believe we must check this anomaly out for ourselves," Around the room, heads nodded. "We don't want the others to get the first." Ganesh looked grim. He didn't want the D-day attack to happen again.

Arjun sighed, jawline hardening. Why did the damn ship have to come under his leadership? His eyes hardened as his resolve strengthened.

"To Antarctica then!"

CHAPTER EIGHT

"Reports suggest that the UFO has landed at Antarctica."

Richard Grey said as he stared at the camera before him. Richard had worked for the BBC like his granddad before him. When the camera switched to replay the footage of the ship, he mopped his brow with a white handkerchief. He gulped a huge glass of water and took a deep breath. Today was his first day as news anchor and he was freaking out with the story of the ship. They had contacted a professor at Stanford to help them. His producer Brian signaled him to get ready as the professor had come online. The camera switched back to Richard as he donned his trademark smile.

"Welcome back. We're now joined by Professor King from the University of Stanford. Hello Prof."

"Hello Richard. Nice to hear from you again." The professor said, his face being projected onto the screen. The background featured a massive demonstration by some selected Christians denouncing the ship as a hoax and a ploy by scientist to discredit the church.

"Let me cut to the chase," Richard said as he turned to face the professor. "Is this an alien ship?"

Professor King smiled, obviously amused by the question. "Now, Richard that's a rather interesting theory. So far as I can tell you the ship did not originate from any country. It simply appeared out of nowhere."

"But Prof, how is that possible? With the technology we have today shouldn't we have been able to spot it?"

"Richard, I'm a scientist. I cannot speculate on the origins of this ship but all I can say is that at the moment we do not have enough information on the origins of the ship."

"But in all honestly do you think it's an alien ship?"

"We are not excluding any possibility."

"Forgive me Prof, but do you think this ship is somehow related to the..." Richard looked towards his producer Brian for confirmation.

The subject he was about to broach was something forbidden in media circles. The professor seemed to understand his difficulty and weighed in.

"Richard, I can tell you this for certain. We have no evidence to suggest at this time that the ship is in any way connected to our history. But I believe we must be cautious in excluding any possibility."

"Thank you for your time, Prof." Richard said as the professor's screen blacked out. "We will keep you updated cherished viewers as this strange event unfolds."

CHAPTER NINE

Greg Wilson stared at the stacks of books piled on his work station. It had been two days since the mysterious ship had landed at Antarctica. Those two days had been hectic at NASA. They were doing everything they could to trace the origins of the ship. Greg had browsed through numerous footages of the ship trying to pinpoint the exact location of the ship's entry. So far nothing. He squeezed his eyes and grabbed his coffee to drink when he realized it was empty. He cursed. Around him, similarly haggard looking faces were busy on their computers. It had been momentous when the ship had been sighted but with the Americans, Russians and other countries racing towards Antarctica, it had become a desperate mission to find out more about the ship. Why did the ship have to come at this time? He squeezed his eyes, reclining into his chair. The polar caps were gone, entire species had gone extinct. It was almost as if the planet was dying. Some said covid-19 had accelerated the decimation of human kind. But Greg doubted it yet a part of him knew that part of history was not a fabrication. How a virus could decimate millions of people had been unheard off? The short nuclear war had worsened matters when the world was recovering from the threat of the virus. Greg glanced at the picture of Greta Thunberg, a historical figure from the past. She was partly right. Yet why didn't people listen then? Climate change was not a myth as some had believed centuries ago. Things had quickly escalated after the D-day attack. With tsunamis and dormant volcanoes spewing ash and smoke into the sky, no wonder extinction activists were actively demonstrating across the world. Some places in Africanus had perpetual storms raging over there. Governments were finding it difficult to even control the population.

Greg sighed and starred at the grainy shot of the ship. He scratched his head pondering why the ship landed at Antarctica. He tapped his desk with his forefinger as he chewed his lower lip. His mind sped back to some of the old movies he used to watch. He recalled one, Independence Day. Gosh! He had enjoyed those movies. The ship was giving off a certain signal which he failed to comprehend. He realized that he was tapping a rhythm with his fore finger when a strange idea popped into his mind. He latched onto his keyboard. How would an intelligent being from another planet communicate with them? He began to type furiously hitting each stroke hard. Some of his colleagues got nearer, mystified by his sudden agitation. He isolated the different signals the ship was giving and narrowed down on one. He frowned when the same pattern of radio waves seemed to repeat itself.

"That's impossible." Greg said in disbelief as he stared at the pattern repeating itself. A hush had come over every one. He synthesized the waves using an application NASA used for deep space signals. He head gasps behind him as blood drained from his face.

"Oh God!"

CHAPTER TEN

General Dwight Johnson of the Space force command stood rigid, a phone held to one ear as he listened to the president on the other line. His hand fisted beside him as he nodded in the affirmative.

"Yes, Madam President." He gritted his teeth, a man unused to receiving orders from a woman. He slammed the phone down, nostrils flaring. "Bloody politicians who think they can do the fucking job." His men chuckled. Before them was a hologram of the ship surrounded by a force field. One of his men, a dark skinned man, pointed towards the hologram

"Analysis reveals that the shield cannot be penetrated with force but I believe sound waves can travel through." The tech guy said, a frown on his face. A soldier rushed into the command tent alarming the occupants. The general's hand went to his sidearm.

"Sir, we have company."

The general rushed out together with his men. He took a binocular from a soldier.

"Oh! Bugger! Look sharp men!" he roared as several soldiers perked up, grabbing weapons and turning on the spotlights.

COMMANDER MATTHEW ASSAN of the Black Federation stood akimbo in front of the war plane as his men got down carrying arms and gunships rolling off the ship. He wound the black cloth tightly around his neck as his breath frosted before him. Every part of him wished he was home even if there was nothing to return to. The former African nations now Africanus had been the least attacked in the D-day attack yet a hundred years after the attack, they had not fared any better. If there was one thing worrying him, it was the sight of the American forces on the north side of the ship. He spied a blonde man with binoculars looking straight at him. He had his orders to secure the ship by whatever means necessary. He turned round and barked orders to his men to ready their weapons. They were not going without a fight. He took a cigarette from his pack and lit it. He dragged deeply savoring the taste and relishing it. They were a rare commodity now. He ground the butt under his heel and took his sidearm out. He heard a commotion to his left and frowned. Another military aircraft was alighting at the west side. His jawline hardened. It was going to be a long standoff.

"Get me a megaphone!" he snapped at one of his men in his thick Ghanaian accent.

PRIME MINISTER ARJUN Singh stood behind the monitors in the crisis room as live footage from his men disembarking on the west side of the ship played across the screen. Information reaching him indicated the Americans and Africanus had already arrived at Antarctica. Each had landed a few miles from the ship. The ship's active force field prevented anyone from approaching. The ship had garnered much attention from the media. It was a welcome respite from the troubling woes of the planet. With resources in short supply, it had turned into a survival of the fittest. Arjun Singh knew his grip on power was weakening. It was no fault of his but when half of the population was starving due to circumstances beyond his control, there was little a prime minister could do. Maybe the mysterious ship would provide answers. The footage veered upwards as lights were seen in the skies.

Arjun felt his hope dampening. "Which country is that?"

"The Arab nations, prime minister." Someone said.

Arjun gripped a chair to steady himself. Things were escalating too quickly. Many had blamed the Arab nations for the D-day attack especially the Iranians. No one had counted on them unifying. Arjun knitted his bushy eyebrows trying to come up with a plausible explanation for the Arabs to be involved in this.

"Are our men ready?" He asked as the footage on the screen showed the Indian men getting into position. A silence had descended over the room like a calm in the storm. Someone gasped.

"The Russians are landing on the East side sir,"

"What!"

Arjun felt his undergarment cling to his back. The room was chilled yet he felt hot. Five blocs of the world superpowers in one place was a bad omen. He felt his stomach drop. He stared at the footage of the ship. It was like a bad dream. There was no choice; he had to see this through to the end even if the outcome was distasteful.

"Inform our men to get ready." Arjun said as bile rose to his mouth.

CHAPTER ELEVEN

The ship stood silent in the night enshrouded by the flood of lights from the helicopters and ships surrounding it. No country had yet made any move. With Antarctica being nobody's land, none had laid claim to the ship since contact had not being made. A wiser decision would have been to collaborate and secure the ship yet distrust and animosity after the D-day attack had permanently put all countries on red alert. Each was strategizing how to outwit one another to get access to the ship. The force field was the immediate problem. But that was going to change soon.

Dimitri Nicholav wound his parker around his neck and ground the cigar he had being smoking. He barked orders to his men. And they began to move. They had been assured by their Russian scientist that the plan would work. He could have stayed behind but he needed to see it for himself. Floodlights shone on them as a megaphone blasted a voice into the surroundings.

"Hold! You're infringing on international site." the voice of Matthew Assan carried over the biting winds of Antarctica. The commanders of the five countries paused in their activities. Dimitri cursed under his breath. The ship stood in the middle. Soldiers from the five countries had trained their weapons on each other, their breath blowing steam into the icy atmosphere.

THE IRANIAN SUPREME leader sat in his secret bunker, a grin on his face. He raised a phone to his ear and smiled. At last the infidels were about to be hit from behind. He raised a phone to his ear and was about to utter the command which would see the Arabs turn on the Westerners. Pity the Africanus were involved, casualties of war. On Antarctica, the army of the Arab nations got ready to unleash an attack which would stun the world.

GENERAL DWIGHT JOHNSON cursed under his breath. Things were escalating quickly out of hands. The Russians were trying to lay claim to the ship. Matthew Assan from the Africanus was trying to be diplomatic and failing miserably. The Arab nations were unreadable. They were up to something sinister, General Dwight was certain of it. He had orders from the president. She wasn't Trump but could make his day a hell lot difficult if he failed this mission. Any course of action now would lead to a blood bath.

"Fuck this! Soldiers!" General Johnson bellowed. "We take the ship before anyone else!"

Guns cocked as men moved forward under the guise of the night. Thermal images on all sides showed soldiers from all sides were converging on the ship. Only the Arab nations were stationary. But none thought of them. From his secret room, the supreme leader was viewing from his room and raised a hand, his other hand clutched a phone to his ear. Before he could utter the command, the force field from the ship fell, momentarily confusing the converging armies.

"What the–" General Johnson said, as a red glow intensified around the ship. The pause was but a moment on all sides as they all rushed to make first contact. General Johnson had been a soldier enough to know something was wrong. He took his walkie-talkie to order his men back when a sonic boom came from the ship hitting everyone within half a mile of the ship, rendering all their weapons useless.

Matthew Assan blinked, wiping blood from his nose as he stood up. Around him, similar faces of shock stared back at him. What had just happened? His head whipped around as the ship began to emit a high pitched sound. They all screamed and covered their ears as they hit the ground from the excruciating noise.

CHAPTER TWELVE

Greg Wilson was still staring at the decoded message on the screen when the high pitched sound from the ship hit him as he clutched his ears. All around him, people held their ears, screaming. In India, Arjun Singh held onto a chair as his ear drums were bombarded by the high pitched sound, tears streaming down his face. Whatever the high pitched sound was, it seemed to affect everyone on the planet. Everything came to a standstill, cars stopped as people clutched their ears.

But upon a closer examination the high pitched sound seemed to be repeating one particular word in all languages.

"EXTINCTION!"

"EXTINCTION!"

Abruptly it stopped as it had started. In Iran, the supreme leader was lying in a fetal position, shock and fear on his face. What had just happened?

On Antarctica, the leaders of the five armies stood up, eyeing each other warily, each of them dazed by the event. Their wits returned and the ship was still in sight of them. Each knew the rules of discovery. The first to touch the ship claimed ownership.

"Now!" Matthew screamed as soldiers scrambled to get to the ship. The mass of enemy soldiers moved to intercept each other when a hissing sound came from the ship halting each of them in their stride towards the ship. They all paused, momentarily taken back by the sudden development.

General Dwight Johnson boasted of having no fear on the battlefield but even as he saw the ship's door opening, he felt a preternatural fear. By some mysterious machinations, the high pitched sound from the ship had been engineered to hack into every signal on the planet. Not only were the soldiers on Antarctica seeing the ship but the rest of humanity was. Somehow holograms of the ship were displayed everywhere. From the deplorable states of India, to the fallen great empire of America, the Africanus states, the once communist state which was led by Putin was in the thrall of the image of the ship. By some weird signal, projections of the ship had been displayed across the planets. Even the supreme leader of Iran was slack jawed as he gazed at the ship on his screen. Every single human being on the planet was transfixed by the image of the ship as its door opened and you could hear the echo of footsteps of whatever was coming out.

It wasn't that people were shocked but the instinctive dread of the unknown had people rooted to the spot. The planet was a beating heart of humanity eager and dreading the unknown emerging out of the ship. They wanted to know what was in the ship yet dreaded it all the same. Every heart beat in tandem as they watched the ship's door open and two beings walked out of the glow of its door. The world took a collective gasp part in fear and relief as the eyes of the beings fell on them. It was a profound moment as the last two remnants of humanity looked on their past amid their last attempt at saving the entire human race.

CHAPTER THIRTEEN

Greg Wilson kneaded his feet into the ground as he planted a tree in the spot where the ship had landed on Antarctica. Beside him, other colleagues did same, planting rows of trees. He wiped his face with his hand as he contemplated how they had gotten here. One year after the ship's appearance, the world had arisen from slumber. Some said the ship was alien and the two beings were divine. But Greg knew better. There were no aliens in the universe. The signal from the ship had one word; EXTINCTION.

Greg cracked his knuckles, eyes roaming the once ice covered land. How did humanity get to this point? At least the wars had stopped. The ship had disappeared after delivering its message. Some said it had gone back to the future. But Greg knew better. There was no future if they continued on their dark trajectory. The last of humanity had come to save them and they had died after doing that. Greg sighed. Humanity was on a steep curve. It was almost like the planet was expelling them. He believed humanity could change as the last two remnant of the human race had. He squinted at the sun in the distance wondering why the last two humans would choose to save a dying race. He silently resolved not to let their sacrifice go in vain. As the signal from the last two humans before they left had relayed;

"Humanity had to survive."

THE END

Don't miss out!

Visit the website below and you can sign up to receive emails whenever N.K. Aning publishes a new book. There's no charge and no obligation.

https://books2read.com/r/B-A-WWEE-UIEVB

BOOKS 2 READ

Connecting independent readers to independent writers.

Did you love *Land of no Return*? Then you should read *Pierce and the City of Imaginaterium*[1] by N.K. Aning!

[2]

For fans of Harry Potter, Percy Jackson and the Lord of the Rings comes a story like no other.

An epic adventure.

Welcome to the City of Imaginaterium where anything is possible.

First they must survive.

Propelled from their mundane life, Pierce and Peter stumble into a hidden world.

To prevent an ultimate power from being used to put the world into chaos.

A primordial being stands in their way and he seeks revenge.

---

1. https://books2read.com/u/bW9RWz

2. https://books2read.com/u/bW9RWz

Now the two friends must battle monsters, outwit troublesome gods, answer riddles and stay alive in their quest to find the legendary tree of life and they have only one power at their disposal; their imagination.

Read more at https://www.amazon.com/N.K.-Aning/e/B073BGWBRL%3Fref=dbs_a_mng_rwt_scns_share.

Also by N.K. Aning

Imaginaterium
Pierce and the City of Imaginaterium
Pierce and the Fallen Gods
The legend of Pierce and Peter : The Dawn

Poetry
In Her Eyes
The Agony of Life
A Memory of Death

Short Stories
The Bronze Man's Secret
Jack and God
Jason And The Great Dragon
The State
First Contact
The Agony of a Slave

About the Author

N.K. Aning is the author of more than ten books. Do you enjoy fantasy? Then N.K Aning is your one stop for all your books. Do you enjoy poetry? Dazzle your mind with collections of poetry from N. K. Aning. Do you have kids? Then N K. Aning has you sorted. Delve into his fantasy books for kids. Whatever your taste, N.K. Aning has a book for your taste. He enjoys reading all things mystery, supernatural, fantasy and detective novels. N. K. Aning enjoys watching and reviewing some of his favourite movies.

Read more at https://www.amazon.com/N.K.-Aning/e/B073BGWBRL%3Fref=dbs_a_mng_rwt_scns_share.